THE ADVENTURES OF H(
BOOK 1

HORACE
HORRISE
WANTS
TO BE A
SCOUT

John Hemming-Clark

© Searchline Publishing 2017
First edition 2017

ISBN: 978 1 897864 34 0
British Library Cataloguing in Publication Data available
Published by Searchline Publishing, Searchline House,
Holbrook Lane, Chislehurst, Kent, BR7 6PE, UK

Tel & Fax: 020 8295 0739
www.inyougo.webeden.co.uk

Printed by: www.catfordprint.co.uk

For Susie – who sent me off to scouts for a year and I
never came back.

The stories that appear in The Adventures of Horace
Horrise have been inspired by the scouts of Chislehurst,
Bromley District and further afield, not forgetting the Guides
that we meet at international jamborees and other events
from time to time. Without their leaders who are such
generous providers, for free, of their time these books
would not be possible. So "thank you" to all of you.
Scouting is a great adventure! If you're interested in joining,
whatever your age, go to www.scouts.org.uk and type in
your postcode.

Preface

It was whilst writing "In You Go! A year or two in the life of a scout leader" that it became apparent that there was great demand for books that tell of the exploits of adventurous young people in a contemporary setting. I had always been a fan of Richmal Crompton's* "Just William" series of books with their small cast, led by a boy who used to get into all sorts of bother but usually ended up smelling of roses, so to speak. I felt that more than ever there was, as well as a demand, a need for a modern-day William who would carry the torch for young people enjoying themselves in the open air with minimal disturbance from technology and, to a lesser extent, adults.

Naturally, as a scout leader, I had my source material with the scouting programme built to provide enjoyment and fun, participation in activities - both indoors and outdoors, learning by doing, sharing in spiritual reflection, taking responsibility and making choices, undertaking new and challenging activities, and making and living by the Scout Promise.

I also had the setting for my main character, Horace - a boy who wasn't to start with, but desperately wanted to be, a scout. Horace, like most of my real scouts, lives in Chislehurst in Kent on the London border. Chislehurst is, in the main, fairly affluent and the characters of Horace and his friends are drawn from the people around us with the situations that they get into often based on actual events, but no more than that.

After the dust had settled on my second book, "Sleeping Bags and Tortures. The Private Diaries of an Adventurous Scout and his Scout Leader," instead of immediately continuing with the third and final book in the series, I picked up my metaphorical pen and wrote nine stories focussing on Horace and his adventures. Scouting binds the stories together, but his exploits are mostly outside of scouting events where his comments are unguarded and his activities are not risk assessed.

Too long to put into a single book, the nine stories are being published as individual novellas or novelettes. Although each one is a stand-alone tale in its own right there are common threads running through the nine and so, to maximise one's understanding of people, places and events, I would recommend that they are read in order. "Horace Horrise wants to be a Scout" is the first in the series.

As a final comment, although I started writing for my scouts and those of a similar age, I appear to have ended up with stories that may appeal more to an adult market – just saying!
John Hemming-Clark

*As an interesting footnote, Richmal Crompton ended her days living in Chislehurst. Maybe some, just some, of William's breath has been swallowed by Horace.

THE ADVENTURES OF HORACE HORRISE

Horace Horrise wants to be a Scout

Horace Horrise reached eleven years of age and still hadn't become a scout. He was, to put it mildly, desperate. Apparently there were no vacancies locally, but Horace couldn't understand how just one more little boy would make any great difference. His brother, Sam, had not long become an explorer scout and Horace suggested to him that he could just take up Sam's vacated place in the scout section, but was told, "It doesn't work like that." He had even taken to praying, "Dear God, Please find me a scout place. Amen" every evening, as his mother tucked him up in bed for the night but to no avail: no one appeared to be listening.

The desire to become a scout hadn't always been so strong, but during the long summer holidays Horace decided to follow his father's example. Mr Horrise had recently pronounced that there are "things that are more important in life..." Whilst Sam had risen up through the ranks of beaver, cub, scout and, at the time, soon to be explorer, Horace, the previous year, had maintained that he didn't have time for "all that dib, dib, dob nonsense." The world of a ten-year-old boy was often just so busy, and this was especially so in Horace's case that previous summer. From the time that he woke up each morning to when he finally went to bed there was just too much going on. Even when Horace finally crawled into bed at the end of the day and his mother had kissed him goodnight, there was still another hour or so of activity above, or occasionally below, the sheets. Sometimes the activity took place above and below, both at the same time, such as when Horace's torch was involved.

His was no ordinary torch. It was one to match any scout torch for sure. It could certainly shine a great light, which was particularly useful for such a piece of equipment, but there was so much more. There was a light with not only three varying degrees of intensity, but the light could also be zoomed in or out, as well as flash - slow to fast - or even SOS. The best bedroom game to be played, especially as summer gave way to autumn which gave way to winter, and often during a new moon when it was very, very dark outside, was with the torch switched to fast flash. Horace could have played this best game more often if he left the curtains alone, but he didn't so he couldn't. Although Horace's mother would close his curtains every evening when saying "goodnight," the first thing that he would do, once she had quietly left his room, was jump out of bed and open them again. This would mean that his mother, every morning, when she came into his room to wake him up, would utter to herself, "I'm sure I closed those curtains last night." This utterance was repeated every day without fail, and was so regular that Horace could lie in bed in the morning with his eyes shut, and know that when the door handle was turned it was six forty-seven. He mother would have awoken at six forty-five and taken exactly two minutes to get out of bed, put on her dressing gown and walk to Horace's room. Once the door handle rattled, Horace would count to thirteen, using the beats of the National Anthem, Daa daa daa daa da da, daa daa daa daa da da, daa daa daa daa... before miming his mother's words from beneath his duvet as she repeated them once more, "I'm sure I closed those curtains last night."

During the winter, when not playing his torch game, Horace would crawl back into bed and lie on his side for minutes, although he thought that it was hours, looking out of the window at the night sky and taking in the moon, the stars

4

and various human constructs that flashed, spluttered and blinked or just shone as they went on their mysterious journeys out in deep space. "Could I be a spaceman?" he wondered. "Maybe even a starman?" He didn't yet know. However his friend Charlie told him during the summer just past that most astronauts had been scouts and thus the seed was planted. Horace had decided that he needed to be prepared - prepared for whatever he decided he was going to do, although he wasn't so sure how he could prepare for something that he was going to do before he knew that he was going to do it. But by the time that he had thought this through this far he had usually fallen asleep.

The fast flash mode on Horace's torch was meant to be used to attract attention when lost or stranded, without using up all the battery in a matter of minutes, but Horace had better ideas. He would set the flash to its fastest setting so that, if he moved his hand in front of it, it would appear as if his hand were jumping around like in an old black and white film. The reality was that he was only waving. It was no wonder, therefore, that Horace should then, once he had tired of hand waving, turn his attention to Sidney, sleeping happily in his web. Horace assumed that Sidney was fast asleep but couldn't really tell as he was unable to see whether his eyes were open and couldn't see him breathing either. He had rather assumed that Sidney was a boy, but he wasn't sure how he could have found that one out without a microscope and some hairspray. Horace's mother, who had an irrational fear of most species of arachnids, had once - in desperation - called upon a can of Silvikrin hairspray to help in the partial defeat of a large spider that she found crawling across the bathroom ceiling just as she was about to jump into the bath. She didn't "whop it one" with the container as her husband had later suggested but instead sprayed the poor spider with the contents of an almost full can. The sticky liquid did the trick: the spider went rigid as if it had been cryogenically frozen and as it was unable to maintain its grip on the ceiling, presumably due to the increased weight that it had been unsolicitedly encumbered with, dropped vertically from its horizontal path and straight into the bath. It landed feet first in the water and, with its raised body, remained motionless on top of the lavender-scented surface like a moored catamaran. His mother quickly decided that sharing a bath with a stiff spider was even worse that wallowing in the depths with one eye on the beast crossing the ceiling. However, rather than retrieve the mummified corpse and flush it down the toilet, she pulled out the plug and let the bathful of water wastefully disappear down the hole. Unfortunately the spider refused to follow and once the water had all drained away, it sat astride the plug hole as if on guard. Horace's mother sighed, removed her dressing gown and jumped in the shower.

Horace was reasonably aware of the differences between himself and his younger sister Olivia to know that she wasn't a boy; he was also fairly sure that he could tell the difference in some of the larger of the world's animals, especially after the embarrassing incident that had recently taken place at Whipsnade Zoo. Horace was fascinated by a herd of Asian elephants that were walking in a straight line through the paddock with their trunks wrapped round the tail of the elephant in front. Horace pointed to the largest of the herd and exclaimed, "Mummy, that elephant has five legs." His mother smiled and, putting her hand on his shoulder and gently turning him round to face the other way, told him that the elephant's fifth leg wasn't a leg at all, it was "his manhood." For a few days after this incident Horace was greatly troubled, lest it meant that human daddies always had to walk around trying to hide their own manhood, but eventually he decided that an elephant was a particularly large beast and most human daddies not so, so it was probably okay. Nevertheless the incident had given him an indication of how he could tell the difference between the sexes, especially very large unclothed ones, but spiders were an altogether more difficult challenge.

One afternoon, in pursuit of confirming or disproving his own personal theory on the matter, he had picked up George who was fast asleep on the sofa. Horace knew that George was a boy as not only was he a tabby, which his mother had told him meant he was a boy, but also because he was called George which was also definitely an exclusively boy's name, or so he presumed. He cradled him in his arms and once George had begun to purr, had started to stroke gently around his nether regions - a place where stroking hands do not usually want to go as this would normally mean immediately after a thorough washing of the hands with hot, soapy water, both of which were an anathema to young boys, would be necessary. Horace, however, did not get that far. He gently ran his hand down George's tummy and was just about to go between his hind legs when George growled - a low-pitched wail of warning - then hissed, then somehow managed, whilst still upside down, to spring up into the air giving Horace a fantastic scratch down his left arm on the way out of a not-very-tight grasp. Horace let out a scream, George let out a "ssssRoww!" and shot behind the piano as mother came running.

"What's the matter, darling?" she asked sympathetically, but without looking at him, instead choosing to see whether she could catch sight of the cat.

Horace held up his bloodied arm under her nose then whimpered as mother, wide-eyed but remaining as calm as mothers generally do - used, as they are, to the scratches and scrapes of childhood living - told Horace to keep his arm raised whilst she went and found a flannel and some Savalon.

"What happened exactly?" she asked once she had returned armed with the tools of first aid, including the best antidotes to childhood injury - a hug and double-chocolate chip cookie.

"George scratched me," he whimpered. His mother wasn't completely sympathetic though; normally there would have been a little smoke before the fire. Furthermore George was her cat, a much-needed companion during the days when the house would otherwise have been empty as the Horrise household went about its paid employment or schooling. (Although, if Horace had his way, schooling would be paid also). Horace's mother was feeling ever so slightly defensive.

"Well, you must have done something to upset him. He never normally scratches," she said as she applied a smear of antiseptic cream. Horace took this comment as a slight on his character as well as an implied accusation. He wasn't going to let the matter rest easily.

"He scratches the door frame," Horace countered.

"Yes, but that's totally different. He doesn't normally scratch humans. You must have been doing something to him that he didn't like. Were you pulling his tail?" she asked suspiciously.

Horace thought for a moment. In some respects that was what he was going to be trying to be doing, had he found it, but he hadn't so he didn't, therefore he didn't reply. Instead he asked, using the language of adults, some adults at least, "Mummy, why doesn't George have a manhood?" Horace's mother thought for a moment. She realised that she had been responsible for his learning of this particular genteelism and so could not now just nonchalantly brush any question aside that included this word just because she wasn't sure where the question was leading. Short answers would be the best.

"He does."

"I couldn't find it." This was more of a statement than a question but she still thought that a response was required.

"Darling, it's tiny. And anyway, if you were ferreting around for it, I'm not surprised George scratched you." Defence was slowly turning to attack. However, Horace was equally able to defend his actions as his mother was her defence of George's. He decided to turn the screw further on the sympathy vote.

"It's not a scratch, it's a life-threatening injury." Horace's mother had finally had enough. A truce was called for.

"Yes, darling."

In any event, Horace was not going to ferret around Sidney, especially as he couldn't even reach him. He was in his web, tucked up in a corner of the coving where no human hand or cobweb brush had ever been, certainly not in Horace's lifetime. He pointed his torch to the corner of the room and, from his prone position, zapped Sidney with such stroboscopic force that Sidney was induced into an epileptic and terminal fit that resulted in his dropping from his web and straight into the waste paper basket (that held everything and anything apart from waste paper) that was sitting on the floor below.

Not all of the victims of Horace's favourite bedroom game had been given names. In fact most of them hadn't. He had not usually let the spiders stay in the corner of his room for so long that he considered naming them. Sidney, however, was different. Horace quite liked him and at one point thought that he might spare him, although eventually having named him, he decided that he was becoming too attached and so had to go. But unlike those families that keep chickens and then, having named them all, find that they can't dispatch them when the time comes, and resort to letting them loose over their neighbour's fence, in the local park under cover of darkness or even, if more anarchically inclined, on the top deck of a bus, Horace eventually had no such qualms with Sidney, even though he had just started thinking of him as a friend.

"Gotcha!" said Horace quietly with a smirk of satisfaction. Whilst his mother thought he was dropping off to sleep, Horace was, in fact, taking on the role of arch-assassin, bringing down the greatest threat to local security known to man, a daddy long legs spider that was now no more. Despite its common name Horace assumed that, as he didn't think that there were any mummy long legs, he might actually have been a girl. But it was too late now. He was in the bin and dead. And now that he was dead and metaphorically buried, Horace wondered if Sidney was still whatever he had been to start with and was now just a dead version, that is to say, a dead boy or a dead girl, or did he - or she - on passing from this world, take on a neither sex and from thereon in be referred to more accurately as an "it"? However, if Sidney was now an "it", then he would have to be renamed as neither a boy or a girl. Horace lay in bed pondering these concerns, which were not untypical for a boy of his age, then all the names he could think of. He thought of famous people, his friends, his family, those at his school. There were some whom he knew who had very odd names. There was a new boy at his school whose name was Apollo. This, Horace thought, was a very odd name indeed but, being the name of a manned space programme, even that was definitely a boy's name. Horace decided that Sidney would just have to become an "it" as he eventually drifted off to sleep, torch dropping from the hand of his outstretched arm as it flopped lazily over the side of his bed.

That deathly evening it was one more down, a few more to go - but the night was drawing rapidly in and in a few hours Horace would be having what he called, "a big day" - carrying out a post-mortem on Sidney in the garden.

In the days following he gave no thought to the magnitude of his crime. An innocent Pholcidae, nestling quietly in its web, drawing in flies and other unwanted guests that were present in Horace's room, was itself now the victim: a tortured, dismembered, discarded, and lifeless "it". Whereas a noisy bluebottle, laying its eggs and ultimately its maggots on a discarded piece of meat on a long-forgotten dinner plate that had been lying undisturbed under Horace's bed for several weeks, would be a worthy victim in Sidney's web, Horace's attention had instead turned to something that most would have considered a friend, living in a quiet corner that the occupant considered his home, harming no one.

As winter gave way to spring there was still no news on a scout vacancy for Horace. As another summer arrived he found himself up in his bed before the sun was down in its; the best bedroom game couldn't be played, even with the curtains closed. Instead he would reach down under his bed and pull out his new prized possession, a periscope. It lived down below, along with so much else that was of the utmost necessity in his life, ready to be retrieved the moment the bedroom door had been closed for the night. Horace's world was mostly under his bed - toys and games, bits and pieces he'd made, emergency equipment, a few sweets and much more. What would never normally be found down below would be items that most people, apart from Horace, would assume to be part of life's essentials - clothes and books. These had their own, if rather small, purpose-built pieces of furniture. Under the bed was the place to go to prepare for most occasions, certainly every adventure, and looking out of the window on a summer's evening was no exception.

Horace considered the periscope his prized possession and for good reason. He had made it, most of it anyway. At the height of the previous summer, during one particularly long weekend when Charlie had come to stay, they had eschewed all form of electronic entertainment in favour of some more hands-on craft activities. Charlie was still in cubs and at one of the pack meetings each of the cubs had made a periscope as part of their creative badge. Charlie hadn't been able to finish his at the meeting but was allowed to take it home to complete it. Rather than sit at his dining table and sweat over it, he had decided to take it round to Horace's and let him do the hard work. Charlie had tried to remember how his cub leader, Akela, had said that it needed to be put together but he had forgotten and he wasn't sufficiently practically-minded to work it out for himself. To add to his woes, in the journey from scout hut to home and from home to Horace's, any preliminary work was soon undone, and Charlie arrived at Horace's house carrying a rucksack and sleeping bag on his back along with a length of folded cardboard that resembled Olive Oyl's shoe box grasped tightly in his arms, a couple of mirrors and some sticky tape. The card already had two rectangular holes cut out of it, one at either end, and the mount for one of the mirrors was also already in place, so all Horace and Charlie had to do was mount the other mirror facing the opposite direction to the one that was already finished, then tape the cardboard into a rectangular shape and the job was complete. The idea was then that, with the periscope positioned by Horace's bedroom window, Charlie would be able to lie on the floor, look into the bottom hole and out of the top hole that was peeping above the window sill. He would then be able to see down Horace's long garden without being detected. However Charlie hadn't completely understood the intricacies of image being reflected through two sets of forty-five degree angles and had stuck the second mirror to the roof of the inside of the periscope. When he looked through the other end on its trial run he squealed, "Horace, someone's looking at me!"

Horace took the periscope and peered through the hole. Someone was looking at him as well! However, given that Horace was now holding the periscope up and facing his bedroom wall rather than out of the window, it was highly unlikely that the spy staring in at the top wasn't spiderman clinging to the wall outside, but was, in fact, Horace.

"It's only me," Horace pronounced confidently, "or when you look through it, only you. You have to mount the mirror facing the other way so that you can see out of the other side at the top."

"But how will I be able to see anything, when it's a reflection? If the mirrors point in and up and out then I won't see anything, unlike if I look at myself in the bathroom mirror and the reflection looks back at me. If I put the mirrors in the periscope at two angles to each other, then the image will just reflect away."

Charlie looked and sounded very confused. However Horace wasn't quite sure how to counter what he thought was Charlie's fairly rational line of thinking, neither did he feel able to explain the finer points of the laws of reflection so he merely held out his hand and took Charlie's end-of-the-pier curiosity and reset the offending mirror. It took some time and more than a reasonable amount of tape but, by the end of the afternoon, they were able to lie on Horace's bedroom floor together, look through the bottom hole and observe what was going on in Horace's garden through the top, which was - not much.

"It's quite good," said Charlie laying the contraption carefully down on the floor, but he wasn't sounding too impressed. This sense was somewhat justified when he added, "What I don't understand though is why can't we just look out of the window?"

"I think it's fab," said Horace, wishing to outdo Charlie in the flattery stakes, albeit for an inanimate object, whilst considering Charlie's query. Horace was clearly intrigued by his new toy, and he was already working out how he was going to find space for it under his bed. For now, though, Charlie's question needed answering. "There might be not much going on at the moment but it's like patiently waiting to see a wild animal from inside a hide. If we just looked out of the window then the wild animal would see us and run away, or more likely wouldn't even appear in the first place.

However, we're now all camouflaged up and so that means that all the beast will be able to see is a bit of cardboard bobbing about and so it won't be scared; we can then watch for as long as we like without being spotted, a bit like having a one-way mirror, only ours are two-way, or maybe even more than that."

"But there aren't any wild animals in Chislehurst," said Charlie, keen to steer clear of any further conversation on reflection. Even so, Charlie was obviously none too impressed at the limited opportunities that the periscope was going to present to the hard-working pair of creative enthusiasts. But Horace wasn't listening. He knew from the peculiar growls, grunts, squeals and howls that he could hear intermittently coming from the end of the garden during the long summer evenings that there was something to be spied upon, whether it was wild or not.

Despite Charlie's lack of interest in this new and vital piece of equipment that Horace said would be the envy of any serious spy - or zoologist, Charlie insisted that he had to take it home with him at the end of the weekend so that he could go to cubs with it and show Akela so as to gain his creative badge before term broke up. Horace wasn't going to argue. Charlie had provided most of the materials, and although Horace had supplied the expertise, even though much of it was guesswork, he now knew how periscopes were made and all he had to do was source some lengths of cardboard for himself, two small mirrors and some Sellotape, and he could make his own version.

It wasn't to be. Or, more accurately if slightly obtusely, it needn't have been. In the middle of the second week following the periscope-making weekend, Charlie appeared on Horace's drive clutching their periscope just as Horace was standing by his father's car, puzzling his next move. "As you did most of the work, I guess it's only fair that you should have it."

Charlie wasn't going to admit that he didn't really want it anyway, so he added simply, as he handed the result of their joint handiwork over, "Look after it; I'm sure you'll have some fun with it," as if throwing down the gauntlet.

Horace not only felt that he should have it, but also he wanted it - desperately so - and he also needed it; he wasn't even going to make it look not quite so obvious by asking solicitously, "Are you sure?" just in case Charlie suddenly changed his mind.

Horace clearly was going to have fun with his new possession now that he had legitimately gained complete control over it. It was certainly going to save him plenty of time (not that he thought he ever had any spare) and a fair degree of additional bother. He had already been working out how he was going to get his hands on two small mirrors at the third attempt. He had two efforts (an unkind soul might have called them "cracks") under his belt already over the past few days but they had both ended in failure.

The first attempt, in the week following on from the weekend's activity, involved removing one of the mirrors from the inside of the bathroom cabinet in his parent's ensuite. The cabinet had two doors on it that opened outwards like saloon bar doors in the Wild West. Once opened, one mirror reflected over one's left shoulder and the other the right. Horace felt that there really was no need for two mirrors as, because they weren't side by side but separated by what his mother called "lotions and potions," it was impossible to look in both mirrors at the same time whichever direction they were facing. In any event, the mirrors weren't any use to Horace whilst they remained in the cabinet because he could hardly see into them given that the cabinet was so high up off the ground. He put the toilet seat down (for the first time in his life) and climbed onto it. He could now just reach the little knobs on the front of the cabinet. He tugged on the nearer one as the door opened towards him. It swung open to indeed reveal an array of lotions and potions but also several individual items that looked as though they were miniature torture implements: files, brushes, clippers, scissors, shiny little packets with "Extra Safe" printed on them, a selection of tablets, some in foil bubble packs with the days of the week printed by each pill, and others in boxes with "KEEP OUT OF THE REACH OF CHILDREN" printed in large capital letters. Horace wondered what these adult pills were for. Why were there so many? What would happen if he took a few? Surely no one would miss one or two? He caressed a packet in his hands as he thought through the consequences of his impending action. The name on the box he was holding was unpronounceable so gave no clues as to what the pills were for. What was the worst that could happen to him? Horace thought for a further moment and decided that internal and external bleeding with his eyes popping out and his insides becoming detached from his outsides and whizzing around like a merry-go-round in his stomach before vacating his body by one of several exits, followed by death would be fairly bad. He put the packet back unopened and set to work on the mirror. With screwdriver in hand (from the junior toolbox under his bed) he unscrewed the four corner screws that were holding the right hand mirror in place and prised it carefully from the cabinet.

Horace knew that he needed two pieces of mirror to make a functioning periscope but he thought that he might get into trouble if he removed the other piece from the cabinet also, even if he could have reached it, so he comforted himself with the fact that the mirror in his hand was at least twice the size of the two individual pieces in the periscope that he had already made. He certainly didn't need to make a bigger one built around two much larger mirrors otherwise it would have been enormous and thus far more easily noticed. This really might have scared the wild animals away which would have been rather self-defeating. All Horace had to do was saw the mirror in half. That wasn't going to be a very difficult job, he decided. He had done a bit of sawing in the past and although the material on those occasions had been wood Horace concluded that mirror wasn't that much different and therefore no more difficult to work with.

He unearthed a large, black felt-tipped pen and wandered down the garden to his father's shed with the mirror tucked under his arm, wrapped up in a couple of sheets of paper from one of his mother's magazines lest anyone should start asking questions. His destination was not somewhere that Horace was allowed to go on his own. His father had explained many times previously that his shed contained all manner of sharp implements - gardening tools, power tools, axes and knives, but Horace wasn't going to be using any of those items on this particular day. All he was after was a saw, a mirror saw, and a clamp. Quietly he turned the handle on the normally-locked door. It wasn't! Looking all around for the presence of he wasn't quite sure what, he crept in. His father was at work in London and mother was busy in the kitchen. She had even asked Horace not to disturb her which suited him just fine. The shed was located towards the end of the Horrise's long garden, tucked behind a small hedge which meant that, once inside, he couldn't easily be seen. However, he wasn't particularly worried if he was noticed. He knew that if his mother appeared unexpectedly at the shed door she wouldn't be cross because she never got cross and that was one reason why he loved her so. In any case, Horace had never seen her go in the shed - not ever. She probably didn't even know that it existed he concluded.

Although Horace had been inside the shed from time to time, it had normally only been fleetingly, always accompanied by his father and usually with the sole purpose of locating a particular tool to carry out whatever task they were engaged in - father and son. But now, for the first time, he was able to have a good look round, unimpeded by his father shooing him out with a trowel or hammer or some other implement in his hand. It was a fairly large shed, larger than Horace had remembered from his last visit, which had been some time ago. There were numerous gardening tools neatly stored in their own personal space against the wall to the side of the shed door. Behind the door and running down much of the right hand wall there were shelves with boxed power tools, tins of paint, a selection of DIY tools, and a large cabinet with small coloured drawers holding nails and screws of various lengths and thicknesses. Under the shelves were a folded-up Workmate, a lawnmower, a strimmer and a shredder. It was all extremely neat, nothing like what the underneath of Horace's bed looked like. Horace tried to recall when he had last seen his father use any of these last three items but soon gave up because he couldn't remember a single time, probably because mowing, shredding and strimming were tasks mostly, probably exclusively, executed by Fred's capable hands within the perimeter fence of the Horrise home.

Fred had been tending to the Horrise's garden for years, arriving regularly but always unannounced to start work on all that needed doing in the garden on any particular day. No "knock, knock, knock" or "ring, ring, ring" was needed as the sound of Fred's pride and joy, his six-splined drive shaft petrol strimmer being fired up under Horace's parents' window at seven o'clock in the morning was enough to wake even the most deep of sleepers. Given that the local byelaws forbade any loud noise before seven in the morning on weekdays, it seemed that the Horrise's garden was always the first to be tackled whenever it was their day for a visit. Fortunately, by seven o'clock the Horrises were awake and at least partially up.

As he peered further into the gloom of the shed, Horace absentmindedly put his hand up to the side of the door and found a light-switch. He pushed it down and two large florescent tubes flickered into life. He hadn't even realised before that there was electric light in the shed! Despite a three-paned window in the wall to the left, as it faced the hedge that hid the shed from the house, it was actually quite dark inside, darker that Horace had imagined - until he found the light switch, even though it was a sunny mid-afternoon in July. Now the shed was bathed in bright, if artificial, light. Looking around a little more Horace reckoned that it didn't look inside how he imagined most sheds to be. He had spent more time in his grandad's than this one. Horace started to think how odd that was. Before grandma died she and her husband had lived thirty miles away and Horace had always been in grandad's shed when the family visited, putting seeds in pots or taking plants out of pots or painting things or sticking things or all sorts of other stuff. He hadn't realised before that the floor of the shed that he was now standing in was partially covered with a colourful burgundy rug, and that there was a small area at the far end with bar stools in front of a wooden bar and bottles of colourful liquid and glasses on a shelf behind. There was even an electric oil heater in front of a small sofa. Horace wandered over and turned the dial on the top of the heater. It clicked on, a red light glowed, the entombed oil spluttered into life and within a few seconds the metal casing had started to warm up. Horace let the heater run for a couple of minutes before returning the dial to the "Off" position. "Cosy!" said Horace absentmindedly. However, this was not the end of the cosiness. In the far corner, hanging from the wall, was a television! Horace's attitude to this discovery was, "Why not?" - the only negative thought he had was that it was a bigger television and appeared newer than the one that the family watched in the sitting room. Disgraceful!

This certainly wasn't just a tool shed, this was an Aladdin's cave, a treasure trove, but mostly a man shed and, by the look of it, it could have accommodated quite a few men. Running his eyes along the row of bottles Horace began to wonder what sort of men drank peach schnapps, his mother's favourite tipple. He wandered around to the other side of the bar, rubbing his hand across the surface as if he were absent-mindedly just making sure that it was real. He found under the countertop a small cupboard. He bent down and tugged at the handle. The door opened and he peered in as a little light came on. Now what was a fridge doing in his father's shed? It was definitely a fridge of some description but not a kitchen fridge with cheese and yoghurt and meat and green stuff. This was a man shed fridge with beer and cider and, behind a little door at the top of the fridge, a small bag of ice. In the door there were some small bottles of Babycham with its leaping chamois logo as well as several Mars bars. Horace now wondered if he really knew his father at all, especially in view of the

Mars bars. Horace was never allowed Mars bars. Never. "Two hundred and fifty calories of sugar so 'No!'", his father would tell him every time Horace selected one in Waitrose when offered a treat. For that moment, all he could say was, "I don't know what's going on in here but, 'Wow!'"

He could hardly take it all in. However, despite the enormity of his discovery Horace realised that he was getting waylaid. He had work to do and, if he wasn't careful, he would run out of time. Snapping back into action, Horace pulled the Workmate out from under its shelf, unfolded it in the middle of the shed and looked around for a clamp and saw. He found a large g-clamp variety and a rough cut saw on another shelf and took them down. He was at once surprised at how heavy the clamp was. He put it to one side and placed the smuggled mirror on the top of the Workmate. With his thick felt-tipped pen he drew a line across the middle of the mirror using the saw handle as a protractor. One thing he had learnt from Charlie, or to be more accurate, via Charlie as it was Akela that had told him, was that saws are often made in such a way as to enable a ninety degree angle to be measured using the handle as a template. "Gosh!" thought Horace. "I'm already learning stuff from cubs and I haven't even started myself yet!"

He then moved the mirror so that his felt-tipped line hung over the edge of the Workmate and, whilst holding the mirror in place with one hand, with the other grabbed the clamp and carefully slid the jaws over mirror and Workmate top. He then started to tighten the screw. Once the mirror had stopped slipping Horace put the tip of the saw against the line he had drawn, held the outer edge of the mirror and rather heavy-handedly pushed down. There was a loud "crack!" and a substantial piece of chipped mirror broke away in Horace's hand. He dropped it in surprise and it fell to the ground leaving the larger section still clamped but with an irregular quarter-circle shape removed. The break had started where Horace had begun sawing but had then veered to the middle of the shorter edge to make, even Horace concluded, quite a mess. Unperturbed he unclamped the mirror and marked another line from the middle of the original line and at right angles. He would still be able to make two mirrors for his periscope; they would just be half the size of what he had originally planned. Horace turned the mirror round and started to reclamp. He thought that maybe the problem had been that the clamp hadn't been tightened sufficiently and so, at this second go, gave the handle an extra twist, just to make sure. This time there was a "crunch!" before he had even picked up the saw. From where the jaw was clamping the mirror a number of lines had appeared as if one had been drawing a huge daddy long legs on it. But they hadn't. They were cracks. Horace unscrewed the clamp once more as the jagged shards fell to the ground leaving a neat circle of crushed mirror under where the jaw had been positioned.

This time Horace allowed himself an "Oh dear!" before looking around for a dustpan and brush. "You'ld have thought that there would be one somewhere here," he muttered to himself, scouring the shelves to no avail. Although there was not one to hand he was very keen to dispose of the evidence. "What would Charlie do?" he thought but didn't get an answer. Undeterred he blew the mirror dust off the Workmate, folded it up and returned it to its place. He also returned the clamp and saw to their shelf and popped the Sharpie back into his pocket. Then he folded the rug up by its corners and dragged it out of the shed. Surprisingly for such a well-manicured garden there were a couple of ridges of long, gangly weeds nearby so

Horace, holding onto two corners, let the other two go and flicked the rug as best he could over the weeds. The shards and dust flew out into the air and coated the ground with mirror - sparkling and glinting in the afternoon sun. He guessed that no one would be rummaging around the weeds anytime soon and Fred probably wouldn't say anything - he would just dig it all over, whistling and humming as he went. Horace then thought that if he could actually get Fred to dig the ground all over as quickly as possible then the evidence would be hidden. He would just somehow have to get hold of Fred one morning whilst no one else was paying much attention.

The following day at breakfast, Horace's mother sat down beside him and said his name gently, "Horace." She wasn't so much getting his attention as preparing him to be asked a question. It was more like a "Hor-ace?" and Horace knew what was coming.

"Yes, mummy?" he replied quietly, not looking her in the eye, trying not to make it sound as if he were expecting a question to follow.

"Horace, have you seen the mirror in our bathroom cabinet?" Horace knew not to tell a lie.

"Yes, mummy," and then to confirm the sighting, added, "several times."

"Where is it then?"

"In your bathroom cabinet," he replied quickly, hoping that his mother wouldn't hear or would at least stop the questioning. But she did and she didn't.

"No, it's not," she countered, sounding a little more agitated. Then in a conciliatory moment said,

"To be more accurate, half of it is." She then went on the attack again and added,

"But half of it isn't. What I would like to know is this: do you know where the half that isn't is?"

Horace considered this rather interesting syntactically contorting question and decided to approach his answer as slowly, methodically and contortionately himself as he could manage because there was, after all, only one true answer.

"Mummy, it's like this. Why are there two mirrors in your cabinet when you can only use one at a time?"

"Well, darling, that is true if there is only one of you."

"There is only one of you - and of me."

"Yes, indeed. There is only one of me too. There is also only one of daddy. However, there is not always just one person in the bathroom."

Horace pondered this answer for a minute. He was becoming a little perturbed at where his questioning appeared to be leading. He didn't want to take the conversation down the route it seemed to be going, but at the same time it was taking his mother away from where it had started - with her questioning - and that was definitely a good thing.

"I've always been in the bathroom on my own, mummy," Horace finally concluded. "Except for when I was little and you used to wash my hair over the side of the bath. But neither of us needed a mirror then."

"No, darling. I wasn't thinking of you," said his mother dismissively. Horace shifted uncomfortably in his chair. He was all for growing up and entering the mystery that was adulthood, but some matters he felt should be left for him to find out about in the fullness of time, and not in a somewhat forced conversation such as the one he appeared to be bang in the middle of at that particular moment.

"Then - who - were - you - thinking - of?" Horace started to grimace internally as he glanced at his mother and then away again. There - he had asked the question, but he didn't want to hear the reply. He wanted her to say, "Never you mind," or "Me and my thoughts," if she had to say something. If only he could tell her that it was fine for her not to answer if he be allowed not to answer her original question. But it was too late. She was opening her mouth.

"Daddy and me."

There was no way that Horace wanted to sit and think that one through but he was, in some respects, a little curious. His mother probably wouldn't be washing his father's hair over the side of the bath, and even if she was they wouldn't be needing a mirror. What else could two people be doing in the bathroom? He then shuddered as his imagination raced ahead. When he was very young Sam, despite being four years older, and Horace had always bathed together. All these years later that would be very weird indeed had it still been going on. However, he and Sam weren't married. But his parents were. Oh no, surely not? And if it was going to be "surely", they wouldn't need a mirror in that situation either. Would they?

"But when?" Horace was desperately trying to bite his lip but it was as if his mouth was on autopilot. He couldn't stop it opening. He wanted to run upstairs and find some plasters and stick them all over his mouth so that if it was out of control at least the questions would come out as nothing more enquiringly than "mmmmpfh, wffff, erwffff." But his mother didn't seem the least bit perturbed or embarrassed having decided, many years ago, to always answer her children's questions and with honesty.

"More often than not every morning and evening."

"But mummy. You can't get that dirty." Horace knew his mother was no slouch but it wasn't as if she was running around all day. Once he and his siblings had gone off to school there wasn't really very much for her to do at home, after all. Such is the ignorance of youth.

"We don't wash in the sink together, darling."

"No, mummy. I didn't think that you would. That would be difficult with just one sink. But I assume you meant that you, well, um, well, you, um, bath together." Horace glanced at his mother to see if, by a slim chance, a hint of embarrassment was creeping in but had no such luck. She leant back on her chair, patted the table with both hands and chuckled.

"Oh, good gracious, no, darling. We don't bath together. Can you imagine us getting in that bath together?" (Horace couldn't and didn't). "It would be impossible. We wouldn't fit. Even if we did fit we wouldn't be able to move around to

27

wash. We would drop the soap and then we wouldn't be able to retrieve it. It would slip down between us and the side of the bath never to be seen again until we got out! And how would we get out? We would be like a wobbly jelly stuck in its mould. You could hardly turn the bath upside down and bash it on the bottom, could you? And where would the water go? There would be no room for the water. No, darling. What I mean is that in the morning daddy uses one mirror for shaving whilst I'm doing my hair or something in the other one. In the evening we will be cleaning our teeth or I'll be taking off my make-up. We are lucky to have an ensuite bathroom, but we don't have one each. Imagine if you were in the bathroom with Sam. You would need two mirrors. You wouldn't want him looking over your shoulder whilst you were seeing to your spots would you? But your bathroom only has one mirror, albeit a big one over the sink, so that's not going to happen is it?"

By this time Horace was feeling quite exhausted. His mother really didn't have to tell him all that she just had. It was as if she were trying to get something off her chest. He felt that he had been the recipient of what some would describe as "too much information." However she seemed to have forgotten about the missing mirror. She was still sitting next to him but as he kept his eyes on her he noticed that she appeared to have gone off into a kind of dreamy reverie. It was as if someone had flicked their fingers and Horace's mother was immediately under the hypnotist's spell. She looked all rather vague, with a dinky little smile on her face, as if she were recalling some past event - one that had definitely long gone but that was certainly not forgotten.

"Well, that's okay mummy," Horace said finally when he felt that it was safe to breathe again. It was obvious that his mother was going to add nothing more to her monologue. "I thought it would be a bit odd if parents bathed together."

"As I said darling, not enough room." Then she dropped the bombshell.

"But we shower together more often than not."

The following day the missing mirror appeared definitely to have been forgotten. Horace did consider trying to get his hands on the one on the far side of the cabinet but thought that in doing so he was probably pushing his luck too far. It was one thing for his father to be shaving over his mother's shoulder whilst she was doing her hair, whatever that meant, but having to shave or put on make-up without being able to see what you were doing would probably be a step too far. For a brief moment Horace had the contrived idea of offering the main bathroom with its larger, but single, mirror for his parents to use in the morning, as this would then have meant that Horace would have had a very legitimate excuse for not washing but the fly in this particular ointment would have been Sam. Although only four years older, those four years had transformed a pre-teen mongrel into a mid-teen pedigree - preening and trimming and spraying and combing and brushing and buttoning and tightening, then repeating the whole process, all before school. To have denied Sam access to a bathroom with mirror would have been like giving Horace a torch with no battery - without one there was just no point.

The second attempt at getting a couple of mirrors couldn't fail, thought Horace, as there was no sawing to be done. As his father commuted off on the train to somewhere in the City every morning his beloved Audi was left parked on the drive. Horace always wondered why it wasn't kept in the garage. His mother very rarely drove it anywhere other than the railway station and Waitrose, so he could only assume that it was left on the drive so that it was in full view of the neighbours. That way the Audi could say, "Guess who can afford me?" as they walked or, more often, drove past. More specifically it could have been for the benefit of their immediate neighbour, Susie, who drove round in a little black Fiat Panda that Horace's mother had taken to referring to, rather scornfully, as "Chi Chi," despite the fact that the real Chi Chi panda had been a giant species, well-loved and more white than black. The Audi had two fabulous wing mirrors that were almost the perfect shape for Horace's periscope and what was more, unlike his mother and her bathroom cabinet, his father wouldn't miss them. Whenever the Horrises were in the car as a family his mother would always complain that his father never used his wing mirrors. "If you bothered to use them you would be able to park next to the kerb instead of two feet away," she would complain every time he had to squeeze the Audi between two parked cars outside the Co-op whilst she ran in for a bottle of wine. "Every time it rains, there's a puddle in the gutter and every time I have to tread in it. If you used the wing mirrors you could park next to the kerb and I could alight straight onto the pavement."

His father was unmoved. "They're not obligatory you know, darling," he retorted. "You don't need to have wing mirrors. It's not illegal to have no wing mirrors and you don't have to have any wing mirrors to pass an MOT."

How Horace's father knew this was the case was anyone's guess. He had never had a car old enough to have needed an MOT. Whatever the legalities of having or not having wing mirrors, Horace wasn't going to let a couple of beauties remain unloved and unused on his father's beloved

A6 and so, before Charlie had appeared with the finished periscope - complete with a spare badge for Horace that Charlie had blagged from Akela for "his helpful friend" he had ventured out onto the front drive armed with nothing more than a flat-head screwdriver whereupon he found the Audi - gone. It was as if the Audi knew that it was going to have its eyes gouged out and had taken flight down the road. Horace walked back indoors and asked his mother as innocently as possible, "Mummy, where's daddy's car?" His mother would answer, but not just yet.

"Why, darling?" his mother eventually replied, without even looking up from her magazine. "Did you want to take it for a drive? Were you going to pop down to the shops to buy me a magazine with all the pages in it, seeing as this one seems to have had a losing battle with a pair of scissors?"

Horace was unimpressed at his mother's feeble attempt at humour, her accusatory sarcasm, especially as he didn't have time to engage in any small talk at that particular moment. "No mummy, don't be silly. I just noticed it missing, that's all. Is it in the garage?"

"No. Daddy drove it to the station this morning and left it in the car park." Horace was confused. His father never drove himself to the station. It was the one thing his mother always did.

"Why didn't you drive it? You normally give daddy a lift don't you?"

His mother put down her magazine and looked at Horace with the dreamy smile that she had been wearing at breakfast the previous day. "Yes, it's true, most of the time. But occasionally your father allows me to stay at home and therefore have a slightly less manic start to the day - not having to throw some clothes on and get him down to the station whilst I'm still half asleep. Especially when it's my birthday or something like that."

"But it's not your birthday, mummy." Horace wasn't exactly sure when his mother's birthday actually was but it wasn't in July, it was in September sometime.

"No, it's not. But..." She picked up her magazine and then put it down again. She opened her mouth to speak, then closed it again. Then she opened it once more. "Sometimes, well, it's like this. I wasn't going to mention the disappearing mirror but because of it your father and I had to share last night and Monday night and as you know, the bathroom isn't that big and so..."

Horace had heard enough. He was fast becoming the receptacle for his mother's innermost thoughts and he didn't like the idea one little bit. "Mummy, I need to go and do my homework," he said quickly. And with that final comment, Horace wandered over to the door and up the stairs without looking back. His mother smiled to herself once more, picked up her magazine again then decided to go and have another shower even though she had very recently just had the last one. It had been quite a hot day after all.

Although Horace's father did not usually arrive home until well after seven o'clock, on this particular Wednesday he was much earlier - it was not quite six o'clock when Horace heard the key turn in the lock and then, "Karen, darling, I'm home" followed by silence. Horace closed up his *Tintin Explorers on the Moon* book, which was as near to homework as he intended getting in July, tucked it under his pillow and crept out of his bedroom and onto the landing. Looking over the top of the banister he saw his parents in a passionate embrace at the foot of the stairs. His father had not even managed to completely shut the front door. Anyone could see! What about the neighbours? What about ME! Horace retreated to outside his bedroom door and called out, "Mum-my!"

There was a slight pause and then his mother replied, sounding guilty as (just about to be) charged, "Er, yes, darling?"

Horace walked slowly to the banister again and leant over. His parents were both standing in the hallway looking as if his father had just come in and formally shaken his mother's hand from several feet away. His father turned away and slowly closed the door. Horace changed his mind. He would put off what he was going to say.

"You're home early, daddy."

"Yes, I am," he replied. "But not as early as I should be, because there really isn't any need for me to work late at the office. You know, Horace, it's so easy to get caught up in busyness that the things that really matter in life get put to one side. The pressure is on me to work longer hours, but the pressure comes only from me. No one else."

His father then smiled a dreamy smile, a bit like the one that his mother had been wearing recently. "What is it with my family?" Horace thought. Then his father stopped smiling, looked up at Horace and said decisively, "From this summer onwards I'm going to work from nine to five. That's what my contract states and that's what I'm going to do."

This was music to Horace's ears. His father hadn't exactly been absent in his life, but neither was he around when he felt that it really mattered, like when he was trying to get hold of some mirror to make a periscope to spy on wild animals.

"Does that mean, daddy, that you can help me build my periscope this evening?"

"No, Horace. Not tonight. Not straightaway. I'm breaking myself in slowly. I'm taking mummy down to the High Street for a bite to eat. Maybe at the weekend I can assist."

Horace wasn't too disappointed. It was more than he might ordinarily have hoped for. However he had hoped that his periscope was going to be finished that evening and was not going to not have to wait for another three days. That was effectively a lifetime away as far as he was concerned.

Horace's father smiled at his wife and started to walk up the stairs. Mother wandered off into the sitting room as his father looked up and said, "Mind out Horace, I'm going to have a shower."

"What a surprise," thought Horace but he hadn't time to dwell on the fact. Now was exactly the right time to tell his father what he had just about been ready to confess to a few minutes earlier. As his father walked past Horace said, "Daddy, I need to tell you something." His father kept walking.

"It was me who took the mirror." His father didn't stop or turn round. He merely asked, "What mirror?"

This caught Horace completely off-guard. Was his father just being nice or did he really not know? "Have you not been missing a mirror?" Horace's father finally stopped and span round.

"No, Horace."

"Oh, that's okay then," said Horace quickly. He turned and walked slowly downstairs, leaving his father wandering into his bedroom to get ready, shrugging his shoulders as he went. Horace found his mother in the sitting room again. She was fussing around arranging some flowers that she had just put in a vase.

"Oh, hallo, Horace," she said. "Look at these lovely gladioli that daddy's brought home for me. Aren't they super?" Horace ignored her question, not that she looked as though she was expecting an answer. He took a deep breath.

"Mummy, it was me that took the mirror." His mother continued fiddling with the stems without looking up.

"I know darling," she said, as if Horace had imparted the most uninteresting snippet of information ever, not admitting to some dastardly crime in the ensuite. Horace was perplexed. He didn't want to alert his mother to what he had just said in case she suddenly realised the magnitude of his crime (in his eyes) but he was curious; more digging was called for.

"How do you know?"

"When I went into the bathroom in the evening the toilet seat was down. I hadn't been in there all day and your father always leaves it up so when I found that it was down I concluded that you had been in there standing on it."

"Mummy, I'll replace the mirror out of my pocket money." His mother gave what sounded like a little giggle under her breath.

"Don't worry, darling, we can manage with just one mirror in the cabinet. Now then, we'll be off shortly to eat but we won't be gone long. We'll probably be back before Sam. He's gone to football practice. Guard the house."

Horace sat waiting in the sitting room, pretending to read his mother's vandalised magazine but all the while listening for the slightest sound that would confirm his parent's departure. As soon as he heard the general bustling noises that go with the usual inside front door activity get more intense with shoes being put on, jackets going on, perfume being sprayed, keys being jangled, and a couple of "hurry up"s he called out, "Have a nice time."

His mother tottered in and gave Horace a kiss on his forehead, leaving a bright red mark like a large smudged bindi. As she turned to leave he looked down at her shoes. "Her heels are so high that she's going to have difficulty getting to the front door, let alone the car," he thought. Oh why did they have to take the car, he needed the car. Things were getting desperate.

"Mummy," he called out, "I hope you're walking down there with it being such a lovely evening."

"Better than that, darling," came the reply. "I have a taxi."

"That's that then," thought Horace. "Dad's repaying mum for once by giving her a lift somewhere, even though he's going to the same place." But he didn't hear the car door open or close, even though the car was only a few feet from the front door. Horace swivelled round on the sofa and slowly peered up over the window sill. Oh, if only he had a periscope!

His father and mother had not got into the Audi but had respectively strolled and tottered all the way down the garden path to a waiting taxi, a proper pay-the-man-money one. No sooner had his parents climbed in and shut the door than Horace was up on his feet once again. There was no time to lose. He still had the screwdriver in his pocket. He opened the front door and peered outside. There was no one about so he quickly walked out, went straight up to the car and inspected the offside wing mirror. It was much bigger than he had remembered. He only wanted the mirror although it was immediately apparent that he was probably going to have to take the whole unit off, but how? Eventually he decided that the mirror must come off by itself. "Surely if a stone or something hits the mirror and cracks it it wouldn't be necessary to replace the whole thing, would it?" he thought. Horace pushed the screwdriver blade between the mirror and the side of the housing. It was a very tight fit and Horace wasn't going to get much leverage. He pushed some more, just a little bit more, he didn't want another cracked mirror on his hands. The screwdriver had only gone in about the width of his thumb but it would have to do. He pushed down on the side of the screwdriver handle and the mirror moved slightly. He pushed down a bit more - ever so slowly.

"Come on, come on," he whispered encouragingly to the mirror. "I know you just have to pop out. I know you're not screwed in...I think."

With one final push the mirror squealed and then gave up the struggle.

It cracked.

Horace closed his eyes and put his hands to his face. "Oh no, not again."

He leant against his father's expensive car and contemplated his next move. This really wasn't going very well. Then he had a brainwave. Maybe he needed to tackle the mirror in the same way that one tackled a bicycle tyre. He went back indoors and returned with a couple of dinner knives. He realised that normally it would be dessert spoon handles but they weren't going to fit into the back of the mirror whereas knives would. He walked round to the passenger door and pushed one knife into one side of the mirror and then the other knife into the opposite side then started to wriggle them both together. Something was happening, something was giving way! The knives moved further behind the mirror than the screwdriver had done and then, with a satisfying "ping!" the mirror popped out.

Horace sighed and wiped his brow with his sleeve. It was only then that he realised quite how fortunate he had been. So intent was he on extracting the mirror that he had forgotten to hold onto it; had he thought the exercise through before he had started, he would have assumed that when the mirror popped out, unless someone was holding it or waiting to catch it, it would have popped out straight onto the drive and smashed. Fortunately for Horace, luxury-class cars' wing mirrors were slightly more complex than the mirrors on his bicycle. The Audi's wing mirror was in very little danger of hitting the ground because, as Horace soon noted, the mirror was hanging from its housing by two thin wires.

"Zooks," thought Horace, "that was close," as he realised just how close he had come to losing another piece of mirror. Now all he had to do was move onto the next problem, how to unclip his prey without setting the car alarm off. It was at this point that Charlie appeared with the periscope and badge which Horace gratefully accepted.

"I'll put it in my room now," said Horace. "I'll just have to get this mirror back into its unit. I was going to make my own periscope, but I'm not having much luck," he admitted. "I've nearly got my hands on this piece but it's alarmed."

Coming across this unusual situation, any adult response would be to suggest that removing an Audi wing mirror was rather a foolish thing to do for several reasons - cost and aesthetics for a start, but neither of these were foremost in the mind of a boy like Horace. Charlie looked at the mirror and added, "Or primed to explode."

"What d'you mean?"

"I mean it's either going to set a great big alarm off or it's going to explode. I know if it exploded it would make a bit of a mess of the car, but it would make a mess of you too, so it would be quite a good deterrent."

"Hmm," said Horace thoughtfully. "I think we should push the mirror back in, just in case."

Horace positioned the mirror as best he was able, and when he thought it was in position told Charlie that it just needed a little push to get the mirror to click back in place. With his best friend watching this was no time for pussyfooting around, thought Horace, and with one firm shove with his fingers splayed over the mirror - it cracked. As one half of the mirror fell to the ground and shattered, the other half, the half with the wires that did nothing more than enable the mirror to be demisted, slotted back into place.

"Oh, well," sighed Horace, "at least dad will still just about be able to see the kerb when he's parking - if he wants to."

Horace had hoped that his parents would decide to linger over aperitifs, tuck into a four-course meal with wine and then linger longer over coffee and digestifs, but it wasn't to be. "Why, oh why can't the sun go down any quicker?" he wailed impatiently. It was well past eight o'clock and it was still daylight. If his parents came home whilst it was light there was every chance that they would see the damage but if it was dark then there was every chance that they would miss it, at least until morning, and overnight anyone could have caused the breakages. He sat despondently on the front doorstep but soon decided that "honesty is the best policy" as his mother was always saying. He would just have to own up, and as quickly as possible. Whilst his father might not have worried too much about two missing mirrors, one cracked and one broken with a half lying shattered on the drive was another matter. Still, at least he hadn't gone so far as to blow his father's beloved Audi up.

First to arrive home was, in fact, Sam. He came noisily down the pavement on the other side of the road, whistling and bouncing his football. He had obviously scored, which was not a particularly common occurrence but one which, when it happened, put Sam in a good mood for the rest of the week. He saw Horace sitting on the doorstep with his head in his hands and called out to him, "Horace! Horace!"

Horace looked up and tried a half-hearted wave. That was as much as he could muster.

"Horace! Horace!" Sam called out again. "I am a superstar! I am the world's greatest goal-scorer! I can score a goal from thirty yards! I can hit the back of the net with pinpoint accuracy! It's all about timing!"

"I am the world's biggest boaster! I can think of no one else but me! I am ridiculed if not ignored by those around me!" thought Horace as Sam bounced the ball one more time, but instead of catching it in his hands caught it perfectly on the volley with his right foot and propelled the ball at a forty-five degree angle across the road, over the pavement over the drive... That at least was the plan.

"Catch!" shouted Sam. "CATCH!"

Horace looked up then stood up, not so much to catch - football was not really his forte - as to prevent the ball from smashing through the glass front door. He needn't have worried. The ball took a violent deflection off a lamppost at the end of the drive, spun wildly and shot straight at their father's car. Like a marksman aiming for the bull, the ball scored a direct hit on the passenger wing mirror housing and the half of the mirror that was back in the unit was out once more, again hanging only by the two wires.

Sam crossed the road with his hand to his forehead. He could barely dare to look. "What have I done?" he whimpered through slanted eyes.

Horace didn't need asking a second time. In an instant he had realised that he could wriggle out of this nightmare even quicker than he had entered into it. "Honesty is the best policy" may have been one of Horace's ideals, but not when his brother could so easily take the rap. "You've broken dad's passenger wing mirror. And 'cos they're somehow connected you've cracked the other one as well."

"It's all you fault," said Sam staring at the mess and swallowing the bait completely. "If you hadn't been sitting there I wouldn't have been tempted to kick the ball at you."

"I didn't kick the ball," Horace countered. "I didn't want you to kick the ball. I didn't encourage you to kick the ball. You kicked the ball, by yourself, on your own and you missed whatever you were aiming at 'cos you hit what you weren't."

"Oh, Horace," sighed Sam, realising that Horace was not going to take the blame and rightly so. However, he needed some brotherly support and encouragement. "What am I going to say? Can't you think of something?"

"There's not enough time for even me to think something up," replied Horace, looking over his brother's shoulder and down the drive. "Here comes daddy now."

Sam turned round as the taxi drew up at the bottom of the front garden and their parents alighted. "Go and stand in front of the wing mirror," commanded Horace in a whisper, pointing at the passenger side, "and I'll say something to engage them and draw them away from the car."

Sam did as instructed, but it didn't appear to be necessary. Their father walked slowly up the path with his arm round his wife whose dreamy expression that had been so present recently had returned once more, if it had ever left over the last day or so.

"Er, did you have a nice meal?" enquired Horace, far too solicitously.

"Moules marinière and Sauvignon Blanc. It was lovely," purred his mother as the couple walked slowly past him and into the house, not even noticing Sam leaning awkwardly against the car, let alone acknowledging him or wondering aloud what, if anything, he was hiding.

"If I were you, I'ld tell them now," Horace whispered urgently, once their parents were safely indoors.

Horace waited outside with his brother for a few minutes whilst Sam rehearsed his lines. "Come on," Sam said finally. "Let's go and face the music." But Horace had other ideas.

"I'm not facing any music. I'm going to bed to play with my periscope."

They both crept back indoors and Sam called out, not very enthusiastically, "Mum, dad?" But there was no reply and Sam was certainly not going to go looking for one. "I'm going to bed," he announced decisively to Horace. Then he added, unconvincingly, pretending to stifle a yawn, "I really am quite tired."

Sam climbed the stairs and Horace noted that his brother didn't call, "Mum, dad?" outside their bedroom door, which was probably just as well if he wanted to avoid explaining the wing mirror situation for as long as possible. Horace followed him up and called out, "Goodnight mummy, goodnight daddy," but there was no response to him either. "They're probably asleep after all that moules Sauvignon marinière Blanc whatever that lot is," thought Horace as he closed his bedroom door and didn't turn on the light but didn't go to bed either. Then he realised that his curtains hadn't been closed so not only did he doubt that his mother would now come in and close them, but also that he wouldn't have to open them for once in his life.

Horace rested the periscope on the floor under his window. It was long enough to just peep over the window sill. This would be very hard to detect, thought Horace. He lay down, stretched out on his stomach and picked the periscope up slightly so that he could get a good look through it. There was still a fair bit of light outside but not much of it was getting into the periscope so he was having difficulty in seeing very much at all. If only he had an infra-red lens on the front of it! He turned the periscope to the left, to the right and back to the left. Suddenly he could make out the shape of the hedge at the end of the garden, even though it was some distance away. At the same time he could hear the high-pitched squealing of the wild animal that he had been hearing and waiting to spy on for weeks. His time had come! Horace moved the periscope to the right once more and then slowly back to the left. As his eyes gradually became used to the gloom and as he focussed once more on the hedge, he realised that the reason that he could see it quite well was because it was being lit up by something behind it. Of course! It was the shed light! Someone was in the shed! Horace had not realised it before but because he was upstairs it was possible - just - to see over the top of the hedge and into the shed through the top six inches of Perspex window - although what was in the shed was

44

greatly distorted. Then he heard the noise again and all at once a figure emerged from inside the shed, tumbling onto the grass. But wait - there was still something in the shed! Had some wild boar broken loose, managed to get into the shed and were now busy snuffling up the Mars bars? Horace was desperate beyond bursting to abandon the periscope and stick his head up over the window sill for a proper one hundred and eighty degree vista and not a dingy tunnel visioned periscope view but he knew that the very reason that he had the periscope was so that he didn't have to risk being spotted. Then a second figure emerged from the shed and they weren't short and fat and on all fours, they were tallish and slimmish and standing up. They both looked liked grown-ups but one of them was definitely squealing like the wild animal that Horace had heard so often recently. They were now both running round in circles on the lawn and as they did so they moved a little nearer to the house. Horace was not at all concerned because he couldn't be seen, and he knew that even if wild boar bashed down the back door they would then have to get through the kitchen door into the hallway and by then he would have locked himself in his bedroom and climbed into his wardrobe and shut the door so, with the stairs to climb as well, he thought that he would be fairly safe. Even so, he put his periscope down and went and rummaged under his bed for the torch. If all else failed, he thought, he could turn on the fast-flash and "do a Sidney" on them and he'd heard that roast wild boar was very tasty. Now he had a plan and was armed it was time to resume his surveillance; he had to discover who the intruders were! As he quietly watched through the periscope once more he realised that he was shaking. He steadied himself as he looked at the two figures that had now retreated back up the garden slightly when all of a sudden he realised that they were not boar, they were humans and they were not only humans but naked ones!

This gave Horace quite a shock to say the least, used as he was to nothing more sinisterly undressed than an Asian elephant, George or Sidney, but nothing like as big a shock as when the shorter of the two figures turned round and Horace saw that it was -

"Mummy!"

Horace dropped the periscope and from his prone position under the window sill reached up and slowly tugged at the curtains to close them. The irony of his drawing his curtains for the first time in his life to prevent him from looking at something when at every other opportunity he would be opening them actually to attempt to look at something was not lost on him. No time for a face wash or teeth clean, he was going to get into bed and close his eyes as tightly as he could. He had hoped against hope that he was having a weird dream and that everything would be normal in the morning. He wasn't, but it was.

Horace came down the stairs after a fitful night's sleep, having been woken by the smell of scrambled eggs, not knowing quite what he would find. But all was well. His mother had been into his room at her usual time and opened his curtains. This had caused her some confusion because she had found them closed but she didn't remember closing them the night before; for once she didn't say anything - she wasn't too sure what to say. It seemed to her that when she did draw them they mysteriously opened themselves but the one night that she didn't draw them she finds them drawn in the morning. She didn't think she was going mad but wouldn't investigate curtaingate any further lest something sinister was in the air. Horace was having similar feelings. What Horace found was normality, far too much normality. The other four family members were sitting round the table quietly eating cereal and scrambled eggs on toast behaving, to Horace's mind, like a nervous family does in an unfamiliar bed and breakfast. The landlady would come bustling over with plates laden with a full English each and break the funereal silence with a "Did everyone sleep well last night?" Horace imagined the husband would look up and say, "Yes thank-you, once we had been midnight skinny-dipping in the pool; I hope you didn't see us!" Horace's mother was in her dressing gown, his father was dressed for the City and Sam and Olivia were all but ready for school. Sam didn't look up: he remained staring into his cereal. Their father spoke first, "Morning, Horace."

"You'll be late for work, dad," said Horace, desperate to avoid any eye-contact, but when that failed, any conversation of any description. If his father wanted to enter the confessional Horace wished that he would just get on with it, or not bother at all, certainly not preceded by a bit of contrived small-talk.

"No, no, no. New regime," said his father. "Don't have to get in too early. Your mother needed a rest. I'll drive myself to the station."

"Again?!" thought Horace, but he replied silent on the matter. Maybe his mother had suddenly lost her driving licence and didn't want to admit it.

It appeared that midnight romps weren't on his father's radar, but Horace had another pressing issue to address. He knew that that moment was right, almost too right; he knew that the moment may never come again. He also realised that in five minutes his father would find out for himself anyway. "About the car, dad."

47

His father looked up, but so did Sam. In fact Sam not only looked up, but his face reddened and he coughed nervously. Sam tried to shake his head at Horace without his parents noticing; he tried to say "NO!" without his parents hearing. The front of his immaculately gelled hair that normally stayed stuck to the top of his forehead, even when playing football, fell down over one eye: he made no attempt to reposition it.

"Yes, Horace?" His father spoke enquiringly as he looked up, smiling.

"There's been a bit of an accident," said Horace immediately realising that it was he who was the one guilty of small-talk.

"Drove it into a lamppost did we?" asked his father, far too perceptively for the boys' liking, although slightly wide of the mark. At least he was wrong about any implied damage to a lamppost, apart from a muddy football print.

"I've got to go to school," interjected Sam getting up from his half-eaten bowl of cereal.

"No eggs, darling?" asked his mother. "You love scrambled eggs."

"Sort of daddy," said Horace as Sam moved rather too quickly for breakfast-time. As Sam reached the kitchen door he heard Horace say,

"I'm sorry daddy, but I've broken both the wing mirrors." Sam stopped, frowned, but then decided to continue putting space between himself and the breakfast table.

"Oh, don't worry," said his father cheerily, "We can soon get those replaced. I'll pop down to the garage on Saturday. They'll be able to sort it out whilst I wait. We don't want mother getting wet feet outside the Co-op do we children?" Horace looked nervously at his mother; she was smiling.

"I owe you, I owe you big time," said Sam who was hovering inside the front door with his hand on the latch, and who had been ready to scarper, but who was now looking ever so slightly more relaxed as Horace emerged from the kitchen. Horace started to climb the stairs, then he turned and replied, "Yes. Yes, you do."

"How did you know that dad wasn't going to go mad?" Sam asked, incredulously.

"I just sort of knew," said Horace soothingly. "'It's all about timing', isn't that what you said, remember?"

"I get you anything, anything. Anything you want I'll get," said Sam. "I thought I was going to be dead five minutes ago, but I'm not and it's all down to you. I won't say it again, but 'thank you'. What do you want? I'll get it for you. Anything." Sam was putty in Horace's hands. Horace stopped on the stairs, turned round and sat down. His eyes were almost level with his brother's and the world was at his feet, almost literally.

"Right now I want something more than ever in the world that even you can't get hold of."

"What is it, what is it?" asked Sam. "I'll promise I'll try my hardest to see what I can do for you. Nothing's impossible. That's what the door said in 'Alice in Wonderland'."

"I just want to be a scout, that's all," said Horace quietly, then burst into tears.

***

Book Two is the next in The Adventures of Horace Horrise series: Horace Horrise gets Lost.

ALSO AVAILABLE BY JOHN HEMMING-CLARK

In You Go!
A Year or Two in the Life of a Scout Leader
Paperback: £9.99 ISBN: 978 1 897864 26 5
"...this is one of the funniest books I have ever read." Amazon review

Sleeping Bags & Tortures.
The Private Diaries of an Adventurous Scout & his Scout Leader
Paperback £9.99 ISBN 9781897864326
Hardback £16.99 ISBN 9781897864302
A brilliant book, I couldn't put it down. By presenting the story through the eyes of both a Scout and their Leader you get a great insight into the crazy adventures of the 3rd Chislehurst Scout Troop..." Amazon review

1000 Fantastic Scout Games
Paperback £9.99 ISBN 9781897864296
"Great book, fantastic to have so many games to hand ..."
"A lot of new ideas covering indoor and outdoor games with easy to follow instructions. I highly recommend this to any Scout or play groups and is suitable for all sections and ages." Amazon reviews

Available online from www.inyougo.webeden.co.uk or (inc. download)
www.amazon.co.uk.
Cards: Tel: 020 8468 7945, or
Cheques: ("Searchline Publishing") Searchline House,
1A Holbrook Lane, Chislehurst, BR7 6PE